Connect is published by Stone Arch Books
A Capstone Imprint
1710 Roe Crest Drive
North Mankato, Minnesota 56003
www.capstonepub.com

Library of Congress Cataloging-in-Publication Data
Gunderson, Jessica, author.
  A Rebel among Redcoats: a Revolutionary War novel / by Jessica Gunderson ; cover illustration by Anthony J Foti.
       pages cm. — (The Revolutionary War)
  Summary: In 1780 South Carolina thirteen-year-old Maggie believes in the American cause, but after her father is seized by the British she is forced to live with her loyalist aunt in Charles Town—but when the British capture the city Maggie is determined to get information to Colonel Francis Marion.
  ISBN 978-1-4342-9701-3 (library binding) — ISBN 978-1-4342-9702-0 (pbk.)
1. Marion, Francis, 1732–1795—Juvenile fiction. 2. Teenage girls—Juvenile fiction. 3. Courage—Juvenile fiction. 4. Charleston (S.C.)—History—Revolution, 1775–1783—Juvenile fiction. 5. South Carolina—History—Revolution, 1775–1783—Juvenile fiction. [1. Marion, Francis, 1732–1795—Fiction. 2. Courage—Fiction. 3. Charleston (S.C.)—History—Revolution, 1775–1783—Fiction. 4. South Carolina—History—Revolution, 1775–1783—Fiction.] I. Foti, Anthony J., illustrator. II. Title.
PZ7.G963Re 2015
  813.6—dc23   2014027277

Designer:
Veronica Scott

Cover Illustration:
Tony Foti

Printed in China.
092014 008472RRDS15

A REBEL
Among
REDCOATS
A Revolutionary War Novel

by Jessica Gunderson

CHAPTER 1

THE COLOR
OF THE ENEMY

OCTOBER, 1779
BELLE OAK PLANTATION, COOPER RIVER, SOUTH CAROLINA

The deep, sweet smell of the Cooper River flooded my nostrils. Home. At last I was home.

The wagon trembled beneath me, and I clutched my seat as we turned onto a small dirt path. Before me, wide, watery rice fields stretched far as I could see.

"Look, Maggie," my father said. "This is your future."

"A grander future I could never imagine," I told him. "It's good to be home."

That morning, I'd begged to come along with him on his daily rounds of the fields. He'd been reluctant, which surprised me. I'd just returned to Belle Oak after a long summer in Charles Town,* and Father knew I was longing to see the gardens and the fields.

Ever since I could remember, my father took me with him on his rounds of the fields. I was his only child, and my father promised I'd inherit the plantation someday, even though I was a girl.

I wasn't exactly a normal girl, though. I hated my daily lessons in handwriting, music, and dance. And I hated being shut up in the house, surrounded by thick walls. I'd much rather be traipsing about the plantation with my father.

Worse, I hated the summers we spent in Charles Town. Like many other planters, we escaped the low-country summer heat and mosquitoes by moving to our city home in Charles Town. But in truth, I felt more suffocated in Charles Town than I ever would in the country humidity.

I spent much of the summer at my Aunt Kate's house. She made me suffer through social events and afternoon tea, determined to teach me to be a proper lady. She felt it was her responsibility. I was, as she put it, a "motherless orphan."

* Charleston, South Carolina, was known as Charles Town from its founding in 1680 until the end of the Revolutionary War in 1783, when the city's name was shortened.

"I'm not an orphan at all!" I'd exclaim, louder than a proper lady should. "I have Father."

Aunt Kate would sigh. "Exactly my point, Margaret."

My mother died shortly after I was born, so I never knew her. Kate, my mother's sister, was a wealthy young widow with no children of her own. We were a perfect match, or so it seemed. I loved her, I truly did, but her constant nagging was tiring.

Last summer, I'd turned thirteen, and Aunt Kate was more persistent than ever. I spent hours in her drawing room learning to stitch and to curtsy. "Like a royal lady," Kate told me.

"Royal lady?" I'd spat. "Soon we shall be free of the British and their royal ways!"

Kate shrugged. "Dear mercy," she said, "the ideas your father puts into your head!"

My father held Patriot beliefs, but Aunt Kate remained loyal to the British. She blamed the Northerners for causing a fuss. "We are much better off under King George's rule," she often said. And she always followed her words with, "But ladies shouldn't concern themselves with war."

My only relief during those summers was my friend William, an apprentice at Thornton's Cabinet Shop. William was my age and he never expected me to act like a lady. He spoke to me as honest as he would if I were a boy.

Finally, after many grueling months in Charles Town, I was home at Belle Oak Plantation.

My father had taught me the workings of a rice plantation — how the rice paddies had to be flooded and then drained. Our slave workers fought to keep birds and insects away from the fields during growing season. After harvest, the female slaves flailed, hulled, and polished the rice before packing it into barrels for shipping.

"Perhaps someday I shall grow indigo like Eliza Lucas," I told my father dreamily.

Indigo, a plant used to dye cloth blue, was becoming a popular crop in the area, thanks to Eliza Lucas Pinckney. Eliza was only sixteen years old when she took over her father's rice plantation. She started experimenting with other crops, until settling on indigo. She was bold, passionate, and intelligent. I hoped to someday be just like her.

My father knew of my admiration for Eliza Lucas. "Don't forget she had help," he said.

He meant slaves. Eliza relied on the knowledge of slaves who'd once grown indigo in Africa.

"Of course, Father," I said. My father often reminded

me to appreciate the slaves who worked our fields and took care of our home.

Father nudged the horses' reins, and the wagon lurched forward. "I must take you home now, Maggie."

"But we have been out nary an hour!" I cried. "I should love more time to breathe the country air."

"Tomorrow, Maggie. Today I have business to attend to."

I tried not to sulk, for I knew it was childish. But I couldn't help but mutter, "Your business will one day be my business."

"On this matter, I pray not," Father said darkly.

I glanced sideways at him to see why he'd become so mysterious. *What is the business he is referring to?* I wondered. But Father's face was blank as he stared ahead.

We left the rice fields and trotted through the thick woods that led to the house. Low-hanging cypress branches slapped my face and, rather unladylike, I slapped them back. As I turned to yank another branch, I saw a flash of bright color deep in the trees.

Red. The color that made my blood boil. The color of the enemy. British redcoats.

CHAPTER 2

FATHER'S SECRET

"Father!" I gasped, tugging his arm. "Redcoats are in the woods!"

"Hold on tight," Father warned. He slapped the horses' flanks and they reared into a gallop. I clutched the seat for dear life, my heart thundering. The wagon whooshed along the road.

We were almost home. Any minute now, the house would appear and we could rush to the stables and hide until the redcoats left. "Please let us make it," I whispered.

"Halt!" a voice cried.

A dozen redcoats rushed from the trees and spilled onto the lane. Father pulled up on the reins. The horses neighed and skidded to a stop.

"If I say run, you run," Father whispered to me.

I nodded, scanning the woods. The redcoats had come from the right, and I didn't see a lick of movement on my left. I knew the woods inside and out, and I knew its hiding places, too. If I got enough of a lead, I could easily lose anyone who tried to follow.

And then, I could rush to the house to find help for Father.

"How may I be of service?" my father called pleasantly.

The officer in charge marched toward us. He grabbed the reins and commanded, "Take leave of the wagon."

I scrambled out, but Father moved more slowly. He swiveled on the seat nonchalantly, but his eyes darted about. His hand inched toward the wagon bed.

His lips moved. "Run!"

I darted into the woods. I expected to hear soldiers' steps crashing behind me. But instead, I heard another noise, a terrible noise.

A gunshot.

Then another shot cracked the air. Furious shouts erupted.

The sound jerked me to a stop. I clamped my teeth around my knuckles to keep from crying out.

"Please, not Father," I whispered.

Suddenly I didn't care if I lived or died. The redcoats could string me up in a tree and leave me for wild animals, for all I cared. I could not — I would not — leave Father.

I stumbled through the trees until I could see the road. Father lay upon the ground, and a soldier stood glowering over him, musket aimed at his chest.

Sorrow leaked deep into the marrow of my bones. "Please don't be dead," I prayed.

As though he felt my prayer, Father lifted his head.

"Do not move!" the soldier commanded.

Father's head fell back onto the dirt.

Two other soldiers moved quickly to the wagon bed and lifted the tarp. "Colonel Bellingham!" one of them shouted. "This fine gentleman appears to be carrying a stockpile of weapons."

"A militia man, eh?" Colonel Bellingham strode to the wagon, knocking my father's head with his boot as he passed. "Your militia will never lay a finger on these weapons."

Militia. My heart sank like a doomed ship. I realized then what my father's business had been that day, and why he hadn't wanted me along. He was delivering weapons to the local militia.

Darkness swirled about my eyes, and I clutched the tree trunk so I wouldn't swoon. What would the British do to my father?

"We shall give this traitor the fine reward he deserves!" Colonel Bellingham said.

The soldiers snickered, and one cocked his gun.

I made to break from the trees to shout at them, to stop them, but Colonel Bellingham spoke again. "Don't kill him!" he ordered. "He might have information of use to us."

The colonel kicked Father again, and his head lolled to the side. He must've seen me crouched in the trees, because his eyes widened. *No*, he mouthed.

I wanted to shout at him that I could not stand by and watch him be taken prisoner. But I'd never disobeyed my father before. I stood frozen, my hammering heart the only thing alive in my cold body.

The soldiers rolled my father over and tied his hands together with twine. Then they hefted him into the wagon.

I blinked to clear my eyes of tears and watched them ride away.

When I could no longer hear the creak of the wagon wheels, I dashed onto the road and ran toward the house. I knew a shortcut, so I veered off the road and through a path. When I emerged from the woods, the house loomed in front of me, still and silent. Too silent.

I was too late.

CHAPTER 3

WORSE THAN PRISON

I raced across the wide lawn, up the steps, and burst through the door, not knowing what I'd find.

"Cora!" I called. Silence answered.

"Cora?" I sobbed.

Floorboards creaked, and a figure emerged from the shadows. "Miz Maggie? That you?"

"Oh, Cora!" I cried, running into her arms. Cora was an old slave who'd looked after me since I was a baby. She was the closest thing I'd had to a mother.

"Hush, now," Cora said, stroking my hair to calm me. But I could feel her trembling, too.

"Them redcoats came," she said. "Lookin' for your father. All of us scattered, but they chased after us, catchin' who they could."

I stared at her in horror.

"I hid out in the kitchen," Cora continued. "Thought they'd burn the house an' everything in it. I watched 'em load up the slaves they caught, and some of 'em went off into the woods. I come back to the house after they was gone. I been so worried 'bout you, Miz Maggie!"

My breath caught in a sob, thinking about our slaves who'd been captured. I told Cora what had happened to Father. "I didn't even know he was part of the militia," I said.

"We oughta get outta here," she said. "No tellin' when they'll come back."

At her words, my sobs ceased. I straightened. "I will not leave. Belle Oak is my home." I'd always dreamed about the day the plantation would be mine. But I hadn't wanted it to happen so soon. Not in this way.

Cora fixed me a plate, but I couldn't eat. All afternoon, I paced by the windows, waiting for a glimpse of red.

When night fell, Cora drew the curtains. "Time for sleep," she said.

I couldn't imagine sleeping, but as soon as I lay upon my bed, my exhausted body pulled me into a deep slumber.

A hard pounding at the door jolted me awake. I rushed to the staircase just as the front door broke open. Several men strode into the house, armed with guns. I drew back into the shadows, but one of them looked up and saw me.

"Miss Margaret Tinsdale?" he called.

"She ain't here!" Cora appeared below, blocking the staircase with her body.

"Her father sent us," the man said.

I stepped out from the shadows, and the man raised dark, piercing eyes to me. I knew this was a man who meant business.

I stepped down the stairs until I was face to face with him. "Please leave," I commanded.

He smiled. "My name is Thomas. We are part of your father's militia. You are to leave with us, this very moment."

"I don't care who you are," I said. "I shall not leave my home."

Thomas's smile didn't falter. "Your father warned us you'd say that," he chuckled. "You see, he had a plan if he were caught. You are to come with us to safety. We have a boat waiting."

I eyed him. "I don't trust you," I said. "And I shall not leave my home."

I tried to step backward up the stairs, but Thomas grasped my arm. Another man grabbed Cora.

I struggled to break free, but Thomas had me tight. "We've been guarding your house since the soldiers came," he explained. "And now it is time to take you to safety. Don't make us force you," he warned.

"No!" I cried.

Thomas sighed, then half-dragged me toward the door. I fought with all my strength, but it was no use. I stumbled down the steps, Cora behind me.

The men pulled us down the path to the river. A small boat rested on the bank.

"Lie flat on the bottom of the boat. Don't move or make a sound," Thomas said.

"Tell me where you're taking us," I demanded. "Or I'll scream loud enough to be heard down in Charles Town."

Something I said must've struck him funny, because Thomas doubled over with laughter. "That's where you're headed, miss," he gasped between chuckles. "We're taking you to your Aunt Kate."

A wild moan escaped my lips.

Cora reached to pat my hand. "Better than a British prison," she comforted.

"No, it's worse." I groaned. "Much, much worse."

CHAPTER 4

PLAN OF ATTACK

JANUARY, 1780
CHARLES TOWN, SOUTH CAROLINA

The Carolina sun greeted me as I stepped through the gate.

"Margaret!" Aunt Kate opened the front door and called after me. "I forbid you leave without your bonnet. The sun will burn your face red as a beet. And then you'll never catch any suitors."

I sighed and stepped back into the house. "I am far too young for suitors," I told her. "I'm barely thirteen."

"You must protect the skin when you're young," she said. The sun glinted on her golden curls. "Or by the time you're old enough for suitors, you'll be as wrinkled as an old woman."

"I don't want to marry," I told her. "A husband will just get in the way of my plantation business."

Now it was Aunt Kate's turn to sigh. "Your father has filled your head with impossible dreams. A woman cannot run a plantation alone."

I bristled. "I can."

"Besides," Kate continued as though she hadn't heard me, "if you don't marry, you won't have children. Who will inherit Belle Oak then?"

She had a point. I reached for the bonnet she held out to me and tied the strings firmly under my chin.

"Where are you running off to anyway, Margaret? It's nearly time for tea."

"Tea is a British custom of which I do not partake," I told her, looking her squarely in the eye. "And my name is Maggie, not Margaret."

"Your mother named you Margaret before she passed, rest her soul. Maggie sounds too much like a commoner's name. You are well-bred and of fine stock, not common stock."

"You make me sound like a horse," I muttered. I turned and skipped down the steps, most unladylike.

"Wait a moment!" Kate called. "I shall walk with you. Let me retrieve my bonnet."

I whirled. "No! I prefer to walk alone."

A hurt look shadowed Kate's face. She nodded and closed the door.

Guilt surged through me, but I couldn't help feeling a sense of relief also. I needed to escape from Aunt Kate's prying eyes. Plus, I wanted to see William.

The afternoon sun was bright, and to be honest, I was thankful Kate had reminded me to put on my bonnet. I hurried up Meeting Street. Often on my walks, I turned on Tradd Street to linger in front of the house my father and I shared during the summers. But today, I was anxious to talk to William, so I hurried to Bay Street.

Nearly three months had passed since I'd arrived in Charles Town, but I remembered the night like yesterday. The sun's light was just leaking into the sky as the boat glided toward Charles Town. The city lay on the tip of a peninsula formed by the Ashley and Cooper Rivers, surrounded by islands and, beyond, the Atlantic Ocean.

I had sat up as we neared, cramped from crouching in the bottom of the boat. The steeple of St. Michael's Church glowed red in the rising sun. As we drew closer, more buildings came into view, and I could hear the churn of carriage wheels on cobblestone. The city was alive and bustling even at this early hour.

Charles Town was beautiful, I admitted to myself, but it wasn't home.

After we docked at the wharf, Thomas promised he'd keep watch on Belle Oak and any slaves who returned. I believed him, but I knew the militia was his first obligation.

I'd gone to find William the first chance I could. Aunt Kate did not approve of William, a "lowly apprentice," she called him, so I always had to sneak away to see him.

That first day back in Charles Town, I'd rushed into Thornton's shop and told William all about what had happened to my father. He promised to find out where the British soldiers had taken him. And he did. A week or so later, William told me my father was being held in a prison on Edisto Island.

Since then, though, William had been unable to find out any more.

I shuddered to imagine what my father had been enduring these past three months. I'd heard horrible stories of sickness and torture in British prison camps. Was my father still alive? Would he be hanged for being a traitor? I had no way of knowing.

I blinked away tears as I turned onto Bay Street. Servants and horses bustled past. Ladies in bonnets, waving fans over their faces, moved slowly in the heat. I skirted around them as quickly as I could and rushed into Thornton's Cabinet Shop.

Mr. Thornton greeted me with a smile. "Miss Tinsdale! A pleasure."

"Hello, Mr. Thornton," I said. "I'm here to see William."

Just then, William emerged from the back room. He didn't flash me his usual grin. His brow was puckered into a frown, and his brown eyes flickered with worry.

"William, what is it?" I asked. "Is there news of my father?"

William shook his head and motioned for me to follow him into the back. "Listen, Maggie," he said in a low voice. "You and your aunt must leave the city at once!"

"But why? What has happened?"

"Nothing yet," he said. "But the British are faltering in the North. That dratted redcoat General Cornwallis has set his eye on the South. If he can defeat the southern Patriots, he thinks he might have a chance at winning the war."

Terror seized my throat, and for a moment I couldn't speak. I didn't know how William came by his information, but he'd never been wrong.

"What does this mean for us?" I finally managed.

William swallowed. "You are no longer safe here. Cornwallis is sending General Clinton to attack Charles Town."

CHAPTER 5

HOUSE OF A LOYALIST

"Aunt Kate! Cora!" I called.

I stood panting in the foyer. My sweat-drenched hair clung to my forehead. I'd run, fast as I could, back to Aunt Kate's. Somewhere along the way my bonnet had loosened and dropped. I hadn't paused to pick it up.

Aunt Kate appeared in the parlor door. "Margaret! You look terrible, like some mangy animal. Clean yourself up at once!"

"There's no time," I wheezed, breathless. "Pack your things. We must leave the city. Cornwallis is going to attack!"

Kate raised her eyebrows. "And how did you hear such information?"

I didn't want to tell her. She looked down on William and didn't want me speaking to him.

"William," I said, after a pause.

Kate smiled. "Why, that fool boy is slow with his information. I've known about Cornwallis's plans for weeks now."

My jaw dropped. I stared at her, speechless.

"We will not be going anywhere," Kate said. "And close your mouth, Margaret. You look like a beggar woman."

"How did you know?" I demanded. "And we must leave. We will go to Belle Oak."

"Our place is here. And don't be afraid. The British won't hurt us. They are our friends. And I say, we shall be much safer once the British run out those dirty rebels and restore order to our fine city."

I couldn't believe what I was hearing. The British were no friends of ours. Not as long as they held my father captive. Why had my father sent me here, to the house of a British Loyalist?

I tried to protest, but Aunt Kate would hear none of it. "We're staying," she said. And that was her final word on the subject.

CHAPTER 6

BURNED AND PILLAGED

Word spread that the British were coming. Our neighbors and friends packed their belongings and fled the city. As the days passed, I tried once again to persuade Aunt Kate that we should leave as well. But she was unyielding.

General Benjamin Lincoln readied the American troops for the defense of Charles Town. Sentries posted in St. Michael's steeple watched for British movement. Every quarter hour the church bells rang to let the townspeople know the army was keeping watch.

The chiming of the bells calmed me. Certainly the British would stand no chance against our fierce American soldiers.

One afternoon in mid March, William tried to reaffirm my confidence. "Remember 1776?" he asked me. "The British tried to take Charles Town. But they couldn't. After only one day, they ran off, tails between their legs."

I had only vague memories of the earlier battle. Back then, I didn't care one whit about the war. Not like I did now.

"Don't worry," William said brightly. But his tone couldn't mask the worry in his eyes.

"Something is troubling you, William," I said. "What is it?"

William wouldn't meet my eyes. Finally he burst out, "It's those blasted redcoats! They've been plundering the plantations, stealing livestock and everything else they can get their hands on. Jewelry, silverware, slaves. Burning down the houses sometimes."

"What is happening to the slaves?" I asked, fearful.

"Sold to the West Indies," William said.

I put my hands over my eyes. I couldn't bear the thought of Belle Oak in flames, our servants sold to a far-off, miserable place. Was Thomas, the militiaman who'd forced me to Charles Town, keeping his promise to watch over Belle Oak?

"Some of them are even beating the women

and children. Especially families of known rebels," William continued. "They even destroyed Eliza Lucas Pinckney's plantation!"

William broke off and looked at me. Guilt plagued his face. "Just think what might've happened if you'd taken my advice and gone to Belle Oak!"

I tried to fight down the fear and fury that rose in me at his words. William was wrong. I should have been there. It was bad enough that the redcoats captured my father. Now they were likely taking over my home and all our possessions. And no one was there to stop them.

I glanced out the window of the shop. "The light is fading," I said. "I must hurry home, or Aunt Kate will worry herself to death."

I rushed from the shop without another word to William. I could only pray that Thomas and the rest of the militia were doing their best to defend the area from the British pillagers.

Although the hour was late, I suddenly didn't care about Aunt Kate. Let her worry about me, wandering alone in the city at night. I wanted to punish her for keeping me from Belle Oak.

I vowed to myself never to return to Aunt Kate's.

I headed toward Tradd Street. I would slip into my

father's empty house, I decided, and wait there until full dark. Then I would make my way out of Charles Town to Belle Oak.

I grinned as I pictured Aunt Kate fretting with worry. But my grin faded when I remembered Cora. Dear Cora would be anxious with concern if I left without a word. Could I put my beloved servant through such grief?

Cora will understand, I thought. *She loves Belle Oak, too.*

Ahead on the walk, I saw a group of soldiers coming toward me. I slipped into the shadows of an alley and waited for them to pass.

"The British will be here before the end of the month," I heard one soldier say.

"We'll be ready," another replied. "General Lincoln is dispatching some of us up the Cooper River before daybreak."

At their words, a plan came to me. I eyed the soldiers as they passed my hiding place, taking in the details of their uniforms. I was suddenly glad of Aunt Kate's sewing lessons. I could easily transform my father's clothing into a soldier's uniform. Then I could disguise myself and follow the ranks of soldiers out of the city. In the dark, none would be the wiser. Before sunrise, I would break away from them and follow the Cooper River home.

When I got to Belle Oak, I would find Thomas and the militia straightaway. I'd persuade them to supply me with ammunition, and I'd guard my home, every minute of every day, until we conquered the Brits.

My plan seemed solid. I quickened my step along the darkening street. Most of the houses were shuttered and dark, abandoned by their owners. One house, though, shone with light. I heard shouts and laughter as I approached.

I peered up at the windows and saw soldiers milling about inside, glasses of bubbling liquid in their hands.

"Fools," I thought. "Making merry even though the British could blast us away at any moment."

I resumed my pace, but paused when I heard a sound at one of the windows. I looked up to see a man step onto the window ledge.

"I will have no part of this nonsense," he bellowed. Then he leaped into the night air and landed with a thud at my feet.

CHAPTER 7

UNLIKELY MEETING

At first I thought the man was dead. He lay motionless on the ground, and I stood motionless too, shocked and afraid.

Then a moan rose from his body. He lifted his head and looked straight at me. "That window was higher than I thought," he said, gasping. "I beg pardon, miss, but will you help me up?"

Not knowing what else to do, I grasped his hand and tried to pull him to his feet. But he moaned again and sank back down.

"Why did you jump?" I asked. "Are you a deserter?"

"No, miss. I am Colonel Francis Marion," the man said, wincing with pain. "I could bear no more of that raucous party. In the midst of a war, no less!

But the doors were all locked. So I jumped out the window."

Colonel Marion struggled again to stand. The front door clanged open, and I heard shouts. Several officers rushed toward us. I whirled and charged toward the street, but one of them caught my arm and held me fast.

"Young lady!" he barked. "Pray tell, why you are prowling the streets at this hour?"

"I'm not prowling," I spat. "I am returning home." I jerked my free arm toward where Colonel Marion lay. "Shouldn't you be helping him rather than detaining me?"

The officer ignored my question. "And where is your home?"

I lifted my chin. "Belle Oak Plantation," I said.

"You're a long way from home," growled the officer.

"I have been staying with my Aunt Kate," I told him. "But now I'm returning to my plantation."

"Not at this time of night," Colonel Marion barked. He nodded to the officer. "Escort her to her aunt's. And call for the doctor while you're at it. I believe my ankle is broken."

"I shall not return there!" I protested. "Aunt Kate is a bloody Loyalist."

Colonel Marion whooped. "That she may be, but you're best in her care." He tried to wink at me, but his face was furrowed with pain.

I struggled as another officer took my other arm. But my efforts were useless. Once again, I could not get away.

"Farewell, young Margaret!" Colonel Marion called after us. "Until we meet again!"

His words didn't strike me as odd until later. And odd they were, for I hadn't told him my name.

CHAPTER 8

SACRIFICE

"You met Colonel Marion?" William said, awestruck.

Aunt Kate had not been pleased when the officers deposited me at her door. She did not even offer a thank-you to them, just pulled me inside, glaring. I glared too, unhappy that Colonel Marion foiled my plan to escape.

Cora had rushed to me and gathered me in her arms. I felt pangs of guilt that I'd been planning to leave her.

"I'd never heard of the Colonel until last night," I told William. "Do you know of him?"

"He helped defend Charles Town in 1776." William had an admiration for all the Continental officers. I knew he wanted to join them, but he was too loyal to Mr. Thornton and the shop.

"Wait a minute," William said. "What were you doing on Tradd Street?"

I knew William would see right through a lie, so I told him about my plan to escape. "I still mean to carry it out," I said. "Soon."

William shook his head. "It's too dangerous," he warned. "Belle Oak will still be there when the war is over. And it will be over soon, once we drive out the British!"

I sighed. I'd thought William would understand. I thought he'd support me, maybe even help me. But no. I was all alone.

I walked slowly back to Aunt Kate's. Although the sky was sunny, I felt as though a cloud hung over me. I was trapped under this cloud of war. I couldn't do anything to save my plantation home. I hadn't been able to save my father. I was a prisoner just like him, a prisoner in a Loyalist's home.

As I approached Kate's house on Meeting Street, I saw a wagon at the gate. Two American soldiers stood pounding at the door. "Open up!" the taller soldier was shouting. "Officer's orders!"

I rushed up the walk. I heard Aunt Kate's voice,

muffled through the door. "Go away, you measly rebels!" she shouted. "Take me away in chains if you must, but I shall not help you!"

The shorter soldier nudged the other and said words I couldn't make out.

"I will help you," I called. I opened the gate and strode toward the soldiers.

The tall soldier who'd been shouting turned to me and tipped his tricorn hat. "We are sorry to bother you," he said. "But the army is in need of provisions. We've been ordered to take anything you can offer us."

I beamed a smile at him and twisted my key in the lock. "You may take anything you need," I said.

The soldiers stomped through the door. Aunt Kate glared first at me, and then at the soldiers.

"Do you not know who I am?" Kate demanded.

The tall soldier nodded. "We know exactly who you are," he answered.

"Then you will leave us in peace," she said.

"Come this way," I interrupted and led the soldiers through the house and to the pantry. "We have plenty of food."

"What we need is meat," the shorter soldier said.

"You'll find meat in our cellar," I told him. "And take rice and flour, too."

41

I went onto the stoop and watched triumphantly as the soldiers loaded their wagon with meat, flour, and rice.

"Do you mean to starve us?" cried Aunt Kate from the doorway.

"No, ma'am," the tall soldier said. "But we must all make sacrifices for the war."

"I have sacrificed enough," Kate muttered.

What sacrifices has she made? I thought angrily. *None.*

The wagon was soon full, and as the soldiers were about to roll away, I called, "Wait!"

Kate looked at me, a bit of hope in her eyes. She thought maybe I was about to change my mind and ask for some of our food back.

But instead I said, "I'd like to inquire after Colonel Marion. How is he?"

"He's been injured, miss. Going to be sent out of the city to recover."

I nodded. "If you see him, give him my regards. I am Miss Margaret. He will know who I am."

The soldiers looked confused but nodded.

After the soldiers had gone, Cora emerged from the side of the house, where she'd been watching.

"Miz Maggie, what you done is wrong," she said. "We are guests here."

"Guests!" I spat. "More like prisoners."

Not even Cora was on my side. For the second time that day, I thought, *I am all alone.*

CHAPTER 9

THE REDCOATS COME

On April 1, Clinton's British army reached the Charles Town Neck, the top of the peninsula, and the fierce battle began. From Kate's house on Meeting Street, we could hear the boom of cannons, sounding like distant thunder.

Although Aunt Kate and I stayed calm, Cora trembled with fear. "What will happen if the British get me?" she cried. "Will I be sold off?"

"Don't worry, Cora," I told her. "The Continental Army is fully prepared to defend the city. The British will never step foot in Charles Town."

Kate patted Cora's arm. "We shall find life under the British very pleasant," she said, as though she hadn't heard me. "No one will sell you. For we are not a rebel family," she added, looking pointedly at me.

Those first few days, it seemed as though our army was holding the British off. On April 7, General George Washington sent 700 Virginian Continentals to join the Charles Town defense. Church bells pealed through the air, welcoming the soldiers.

But our delight was short-lived. The very next day, British ships sailed into Charles Town Harbor under a rain of American fire. Eleven ships landed unscathed on James Island.

Charles Town was surrounded.

"General Lincoln should surrender," Aunt Kate said one morning.

We'd been cooped up in the house since the siege began. I was irritable, and I didn't want to hear any more of her Loyalist talk. Before she could stop me, I marched out the door.

A few people milled about the streets, trying to pretend all was normal in Charles Town. I headed toward Thornton's shop with hopes to see William.

The air seemed eerily quiet. No guns boomed. Was General Lincoln about to surrender, as Kate hoped?

Suddenly a shell screamed overhead. And another and another, exploding into the heart of the city.

A woman shrieked and ran right past me, nearly knocking me over. Up ahead, a fire bloomed. Thick smoke swirled into the air. Was it Thornton's shop?

"William!" I yelled. I dodged a charging horse and raced toward Bay Street.

Smoke poured into my lungs. I stopped to catch my breath. My eyes burned, and I couldn't see. I forged ahead, coughing.

A familiar hand grasped my arm. "William!" I cried. I tried to hug him, but he just yanked me along with him as he ran. We ducked into an alley and crouched behind a low wall.

"Has Thornton's shop been hit?" I asked.

William shook his head. "Spared. For now."

As we crouched, breathless in the smoke, a woman ran past, her skirt smoldering. She carried a small, wailing child. I called out to her, but she didn't hear me over the whistle of shells. I stood to chase after her, but William held me back.

"You'll only be killed," he shouted. "And that will do nobody any good."

I leaned my face against the wall. Tears streamed my cheeks. "What is happening?" I sobbed.

"Those lousy British! Attacking innocent civilians," William muttered.

"Trying to force Lincoln's surrender," I added. I'd hated the British before, but to see innocent women and children running for their lives, to see homes and stables burning to the ground, sparked a new, deeper hatred in me.

I peeked over the wall. Smoke billowed from the direction of Meeting Street.

Aunt Kate. Cora.

CHAPTER 10

THE SIEGE
OF CHARLES TOWN

I had to go to them. I had to make sure they were safe.

As though William had read my thoughts, he said, "I'll go with you."

For now, the shelling seemed to have stopped. I hoisted my skirt and ran, William paces behind me.

We turned onto Meeting Street. My stomach knotted with dread. Then, relieved, I saw that Aunt Kate's house was still standing.

William paused. "They're safe," he gasped. He nudged me toward the gate and turned to go.

This time I was the one to grab his arm and yank him along with me.

Aunt Kate swung open the door. Her eyes were red

as though she'd been crying. "Get into the cellar!" she cried.

The cellar was dank and dark, but it was a relief after the bright, terrible burning of the city. Cora and Aunt Kate's servants huddled in the corner. Cora, who was always so frightened, seemed calm as she strode toward me, a cup of rice in her hand. "Eat this," she said. "You'll feel better for it."

I waved the rice away. We were nearly at the end of our food, and with the siege, there was no way to get more. The British had cut off our supplies.

William paced along the wall, seeming nervous. He kept eyeing Aunt Kate, sizing her up.

Kate ignored him and wiped my face with a cloth. "You're covered in soot," she said accusingly.

"Tell me, Mrs. Plover," William said to Kate, "since you're such good friends with the British. How long do they plan to keep this up?"

Aunt Kate stiffened and threw a glance at William. "As long as necessary."

"And what if General Lincoln offers a truce? What then?" William went on.

"I really have no idea," answered Kate.

"You don't?" William thundered.

Aunt Kate bit her lip. She seemed unnerved,

although I couldn't figure out why. "Be careful with your words," she warned.

William laughed and plopped to the cellar floor.

"William saved my life," I told Kate. "There's no need to be rude."

"He should stop encouraging your rebel views," she answered. "Or we will all be in danger."

This time I laughed. "Danger? We are already in danger. Just look what they've done to Charles Town!"

"And look what you've done to your dress," Kate said. "When the shelling stops, you'll go up immediately and change into clean clothes."

I shook my head. Kate seemed more offended by my dirty dress than by the British shelling of the city.

The hours passed, and we spoke little. Exhausted, I leaned against the wall and slept. When I woke, William was gone.

For days, Kate, Cora, and I, along with Kate's two slaves, hunkered in the cellar. We emerged only to check if Kate's house had been hit.

I longed to escape the cellar.

Day after day, we waited for the shelling to stop.

Our food supply was growing scarce, and fear was the only thing that filled our bellies.

Kate tried to comfort us, although her words only enraged me. "Soon the Americans will surrender," she said. "And we can have our lives back!"

"How can you still stand by those Brits?" I hissed. "Look what they have done to our city! Homes burnt to the ground, innocent people dead. And we are practically starving!"

"Whose fault is it that we are starving?" Kate countered. "You gave away our meat."

"They would've taken it anyway," I said. "Besides, if the Brits hadn't attacked Charles Town, we wouldn't have had to give up our food."

The days turned to weeks. On quiet days, we went up to the house and breathed through the open windows, braving the shelling for a breath of air and glimpse of sunlight. But we dared not leave the shelter of the house.

I looked out the window. Weeds choked the bright azalea bushes. The vegetable garden lay desolate and unattended. No townspeople strolled past. Only weary, sunken-eyed soldiers walked the streets.

How long can we withstand the siege? I wondered. I was so weak from lack of food that I almost hoped

General Lincoln would give in. But then I admonished myself for such thoughts. *No!* I told myself. *Never surrender.*

But surrender we did. On May 12, after seven weeks of siege, General Lincoln agreed to Clinton's terms.

Kate and I gathered with other townspeople to watch as our soldiers marched dejectedly out of the city. They would now be prisoners of war.

Then, with waving flags and drums beating, the redcoats poured in, faces shiny with victory.

Kate smiled and curtsied as they passed, but I only glowered at them.

Charles Town was now a British city.

CHAPTER 11

OVER MY DEAD BODY

"We shall throw a party!" Aunt Kate declared after we returned home.

"A party?" I spat. "To welcome the British?"

Aunt Kate nodded with enthusiasm. "Exactly!"

I felt sick at the thought of the victorious British officers dining within our walls. "I shall have no part in such a thing!" I told her.

"You're much too young to take part anyway," Kate said. "Besides, I can't risk you opening your mouth and unleashing rebel rubbish."

Suddenly, I wanted badly to attend. I wanted to give the British my two cents.

I pretended to be deep in thought for a moment.

Then I said with a bright smile, "It's a grand idea, Aunt Kate. If you can't beat them, join them!"

Kate eyed me, wondering if I was serious.

I looked at her innocently. "I will behave," I said. "And I will certainly help in the preparations."

"I will think about it," Kate said finally. "Let's begin planning immediately."

I followed her into the study. She drew a piece of parchment from the desk and began scribbling. "We will serve oyster soup. And plum pudding. And tender beefsteaks."

My mouth watered. After weeks of eating mostly rice, the dishes sounded delicious. "Where will we get such food at a time like this?" I asked doubtfully.

Kate shrugged. "We'll have the party in mid summer. By then, our stores will be fully replenished."

I sat with her awhile as she mused over the guest list and the menu. The study was stuffy, and my eyelids kept drooping closed. "I'm going out," I told her, standing. "And I'll be sure to tell every redcoat I meet about our party."

Kate didn't notice my sarcasm and only nodded without giving me a glance.

British soldiers filled the streets. I tried to keep anger from showing in my face as I walked past them.

I was relieved to see that Thornton's shop was still standing. Mr. Thornton nodded to me pleasantly when I entered, as though nothing had happened these long weeks.

William and I went into the back of the shop and talked about the war. After weeks of being cooped up in Kate's house, it was a relief to speak with someone who had the same views as I did.

William told me about Clinton and Lincoln's agreement concerning the Patriot defenders of Charles Town. The men enlisted in the regular Continental Army were British prisoners. But General Clinton allowed militiamen to return to their families, as long as they promised not to take up arms against the British again.

The news encouraged me. "Perhaps my father will be able to come home!" I said.

"I'm not sure," William said doubtfully. "He wasn't engaged in the defense of Charles Town. And they may still be pressing him for information about militia in the countryside."

"Are there still militia willing to fight the British?" I asked. General Clinton had made it seem like the British now had complete control over South Carolina.

William nodded. "Clinton thought the fall of Charles

Town would subdue the rebels in the rest of the colony. But it only enraged Patriots even more!"

"Cornwallis seems to think that this victory will win him the war," I said.

William laughed. "Over my dead body!"

I shivered at his words. "Don't say such things!" I said. "Besides, we are stuck in Charles Town now. We just have to wait and hope that General Washington will keep winning in the north."

"It's a good thing Colonel Marion was sent out of the city to recover, otherwise he would've been captured," William said. "Marion grew up in the Carolina low country. He knows the land like no other. He'll be a great asset to the Patriots."

I stared at him. "You're thinking about joining him, aren't you?" I said, my heart sinking. Without William, my days in Charles Town would be miserable indeed.

William didn't answer. I knew that his silence meant yes.

"But you're not old enough," I said. "And how will you get out of Charles Town without being caught? The British are everywhere."

"I just can't sit by and do nothing," William said. "I'll find a way."

Just then, Mr. Thornton poked his head through

the door. We both jumped, faces flushed. I hoped he hadn't heard what we were saying. He'd be crushed if William left for the militia.

"I must be on my way," I said quickly and brushed past Mr. Thornton.

As I walked home, my thoughts tumbled with William's words. Would he, barely thirteen, really join Marion's men?

CHAPTER 12

OATH OF ALLEGIANCE

That month was filled with preparations for Kate's party. I hated the thought of British officers and Loyalists in our home, but I was grateful for a distraction.

Kate, Cora, and I spent hours polishing silverware and china. We took down the curtains and plunged them in a tub of soapy water. We scrubbed every inch of the floor and washed each piece of the chandelier.

Kate wanted the house well lit, so we made extra candles. We boiled animal fat on the kitchen stove and then dipped wicks into the fat, let them cool, and then dipped again and again until the candles were tall and thick.

Meanwhile, the British soldiers filled our streets, taking over businesses and homes as their own. And

General Clinton had more in store for the punishment of Charles Town. In early June, he announced that all men and women must pledge an oath of allegiance to England. Otherwise, they'd be sent to the Provost Dungeon below the Exchange Building.

I shivered to think of Patriots from respectable families jailed alongside thieves and murderers.

Aunt Kate, unsurprisingly, didn't hesitate to sign the oath.

I didn't scold her, even though I wanted to. I had to be on my best behavior if I wanted to attend the party.

All of the hard work left me little time to see William. When I did see him, I would beg him not to leave Charles Town. "You'll be killed," I told him.

William always shrugged. "I'd rather be dead than live under British rule," he always said.

The day before the party, I arrived at Thornton's shop to find it dark. I tried the door, but it was locked. "Mr. Thornton!" I called. "William?"

No answer.

I peered in the window and saw the shop was empty. All the cabinets, all the desks and chairs, gone.

Fear thickened my throat. Where were Mr. Thornton and William? What had happened?

As I stood, wondering what to do, I saw a group of

British soldiers moving toward me. "You there!" one of them called. "Get on home."

"I'm looking for my friends," I said.

"Friends?" he guffawed. "You're looking in the wrong place, miss. Your friends are rotting in the dungeon."

The soldiers laughed and continued on.

I knew then what had happened. Mr. Thornton had refused to sign the oath of allegiance. And now he and William were prisoners in the Provost Dungeon.

CHAPTER 13

THE BUTCHER

The day of the party, I went downstairs and found Kate leaning against the window frame, staring out into the street. When she turned to me, I saw that her face was white except for two bright spots on her cheeks.

"What's wrong?" I asked.

"Oh, just nerves," she said with a shrug.

"May I attend the party tonight?" I asked.

Kate nodded. "Yes. But you must not say anything against the British."

"I promise," I reluctantly said, although I wasn't sure I could uphold my promise.

The guests arrived as the summer sun was setting. Kate and I greeted them at the door. Officers in red filed into the dining room, ladies in brocaded silk on their arms. Everyone seemed happy and festive, as though the city hadn't borne a month of destruction.

When it seemed all the guests had arrived, Kate lingered at the door, as though waiting for one more. And then he arrived, a man in a bright green uniform.

He was none other than Banastre "The Butcher" Tarleton. I shuddered. He'd earned his nickname at the Battle of Waxhaws in late May. The Continental Army had surrendered and laid down their weapons. But Tarleton and his men continued to attack, butchering every Continental soldier they could.

Now the Butcher was in our home.

Kate smiled grandly at him. "Congratulations on your success," she said.

I had to hold my tongue. Tarleton's victory was not a success. It was a slaughter.

The dining table glittered under the shimmering chandelier. Rich smells of gravy and roasted meat filtered into the room. My stomach growled with hunger.

Kate seated me on her left. I took my place, realizing with dismay I was directly across from Butcher Tarleton.

I no longer felt even a bit hungry.

Before the meal began, Kate stood and raised her glass in a toast. "To the continued success of the

British Army!" she said. I noticed her hand shaking, but her smile remained firm.

All the guests raised their glasses, too. But I couldn't bear to toast the British. I hoped no one would notice. But when I looked up, I saw Tarleton's eyes on me.

I lifted my glass toward him. "Here's to more slaughtering of the Americans!" I said with a smile.

The room fell silent. Tarleton himself broke the silence with a booming laugh. "You're a feisty one," he said. "You must take after your father." He turned to the officer next to him. "Which prison is Mr. Tinsdale held in?"

Blood drained from my face. I tried to speak but I could only sputter. The Butcher's warning was clear. I was putting my father in danger with my sharp words against the British.

Tarleton laughed again. "Oh, it's no matter," he said. "I have other things to worry about. That Swamp Fox Marion, for one."

"Swamp Fox?" Kate said. "Why do you call him that?"

Tarleton gave her a sour look. "Francis Marion and his militia are hiding in the swamps, attacking our men then slipping away again. I can't seem to track him down."

I tried not to smile as I looked down at my plate. *You'll never catch Marion*, I thought.

A woman spoke up from the other end of the table. "All this talk of war is tiresome," she said.

Tarleton nodded. "Yes, let's not fill the pretty ladies' heads with battle talk," he said.

I flushed with anger, but Kate nudged her toe against my foot before I could speak.

The dinner dragged on. No more was said about the war, and I was bored by the chatter around me.

After we'd finished eating, the ladies went into the parlor and the men to the study, as was the custom. I couldn't bear any more small talk, so I went out into the garden for a breath of fresh air.

A warm, moist wind rustled my dress. I thought back over the evening, and worry filled me. What if Butcher Tarleton carried out his warning? What if he hurt my father because of what I'd said?

A noise interrupted my thoughts. The azalea bushes crackled. Just a stray animal, I told myself. Just to be sure, I crept closer to the bushes.

One of the bushes grew larger. And then a figure emerged, lunging straight at me.

CHAPTER 14

THE SIGNAL
AND THE SPY

I screamed as a hand clapped over my mouth. *"Shh,"* a voice said.

William!

"What are you doing here?" I whispered. "I thought you were in the dungeon."

"When the redcoats came to take Mr. Thornton away, I hid," he explained. "I've been hiding in the alleys. Waiting for my chance."

"Your chance for what?" I said.

When he didn't answer, I knew. He was going to leave Charles Town and join Marion's Brigade.

"You can't go," I whispered. I glanced at the brightly lit windows of the house. "That Butcher Tarleton is

inside right now. He's on a mission to find Marion."
My voice rose. "If he finds him, he'll slaughter you all!"

William followed my gaze to the house. "Tarleton is here?"

"Yes," I growled. "Aunt Kate is wining and dining him, as though he's her best friend."

William nodded. "I'd better be on my way then," he said.

I knew nothing I could say would convince him not to go. "How will you find him?" I asked.

William shrugged. "Marion's men are all along the Cooper River, all the way to the Santee and Pee Dee Rivers. I'll find him eventually."

I hugged him tightly. "Please be safe," I said.

William stepped across the garden. Then he turned back to me. "One last thing," he said. "Aunt Kate is not your enemy. Remember that."

Then he disappeared into the night.

I pondered William's words. What had he meant? Aunt Kate had proven tonight that she was indeed my enemy. An enemy of all Patriots.

The front door swung open. Noise from the party spilled into the garden. "Miz Maggie!" Cora shouted. I could hear urgency in her voice.

I ran up the walk. "Cora? What is it?"

"It's Aunt Kate," Cora said. "She took ill!"

I brushed past her and raced inside. Kate was lying on the floor of the parlor. The guests were stumbling over each other in their haste to leave.

"Has anybody gone for the doctor?" I demanded as I rushed to Kate's side.

"Don't touch her!" one woman called to me, a handkerchief over her mouth. "You'll catch the smallpox!"

Smallpox. My breath caught in a sob. Smallpox meant certain death.

I lifted Kate's head onto my lap. Her skin was hot and fevered, although she shivered with chills.

Butcher Tarleton strode into the room. I looked up at him as he glowered down at me. "Please send for the doctor," I pleaded.

"If it's smallpox, a doctor won't be much help," he said. "You're on your own." And then he marched out of the room.

At that moment, I felt I'd never hated anyone more.

Cora and I carried Aunt Kate up to her room. All that long night, I held her while she shivered and moaned. I didn't care if I caught smallpox, too. I just wanted Kate to get better.

Kate's eyes blinked open. "Tarleton," she whispered.

"Get your mind off him," I said. "He doesn't care one bit about you."

Kate's eyes closed, and she drifted into a restless, fevered sleep.

Toward morning, Kate's fever worsened. Her skin was flaming hot to the touch. I stepped out of the room to let her rest.

Cora was hovering in the hallway, face tangled with worry. "I'm going to fetch the doctor," I said.

When I returned with the doctor, I noticed that the candle sconces outside the front door had been turned downward. *That's odd*, I thought, righting them. Then I hurried inside to hear what the doctor had to say.

After what seemed like hours, the doctor emerged from Kate's room. "I don't think it's smallpox," he said. "But she's very ill. She may not make it."

I gasped with sobs. What would happen to me if Kate died? I had no one to turn to.

For two days, Cora and I took turns tending to Kate. I slept little, and the days and nights blurred together.

One afternoon, I stepped outside for air and saw Cora twisting the candle sconces to face downward once again.

"What are you doing?" I asked. "I turned them

upward after the party. Someone must've bumped them in their hurry to leave the house."

Cora looked at me with fright. "Oh, no, Miz Maggie! Them sconces are the signal."

I stared at her in confusion. "What signal?"

Cora took my arm and led me into the house. "It's time to tell you the truth," she whispered as she shut the door. "Your aunt is no Loyalist like you think. She's a Patriot spy."

CHAPTER 15

A DANGEROUS MISSION

A Patriot spy!

My legs grew weak, and I fell onto the parlor sofa.

Of course. William's words rang in my ears. *She's not your enemy.*

"So that's why she had the party for the British," I said. "She wanted information."

Cora nodded. "And I been helping her," she said.

I stared at her. "You?"

"Yes, Miz Maggie. You see, no one would suspect me. I hung about while them soldiers were talking in the study. I listened to every word. They talked about their plan to find Marion. Then I turned the sconces down, like Miz Kate told me. But the messenger, he never come."

I swallowed. "He didn't come, because I righted the sconces," I said. I flung my head into my hands.

Cora patted my shoulder. "It's not your fault. I should've noticed. But with Miz Kate so ill . . ."

"What will we do?" I cried. "Tarleton will butcher Marion. And William, too!"

Cora looked at me calmly. "There's only one thing to do, Miz Maggie. You must find Marion."

"Me? But . . ." I faltered.

Cora nodded. "I raised you to be brave. And you the bravest girl I know."

I could scarcely believe what I was hearing. Cora, who always fussed and worried over me, was now sending me on a dangerous mission.

If I didn't succeed, William might die. I swallowed.

"I might be able to catch up with William," I told her. "I know where he was heading. But what about Kate? I shouldn't leave her."

"I'll take care o' Miz Kate," Cora said. "Remember all those times I nursed you back from fever?"

I stood up. I could do it. I knew I could. "Tell me what you know," I told her. "There's no time to waste. And besides," I added, "I already have a plan."

I went to my father's house on Tradd Street and returned with an old red coat and trousers. We set to work trimming and hemming the sleeves and legs, each of us taking turns to check on Kate.

Just before nightfall, I donned my disguise, completing the look with a hat and powdered wig. I took Aunt Kate's handgun from her nightstand and slipped it into my coat pocket. Then I stared in the hall mirror doubtfully. Could I pass as a British soldier? I was tall for my age but still small. My lips were rosy and full, and my lashes long and curved. I looked like a girl. A girl pretending to be a soldier.

No one will get close enough to see my eyelashes, I told myself.

I slipped into Aunt Kate's room. She was still hot, her breath heavy. *Please make it through*, I prayed, clutching her hand.

Kate opened her eyes. She blinked. Her fevered eyes took me in. I thought I saw a smile tug at her lips.

Maybe she's getting better, I thought. I squeezed her hand.

"Eliza," she whispered.

Disappointment crushed me. She wasn't getting better. She was delirious. "No. I'm Maggie. Margaret."

She shook her head. "Lucas," she murmured.

I kissed her hair. "Goodbye, Aunt Kate," I said.

I'd told Cora I had a plan, but it wasn't much of

one. I planned to slip past the sentries out of the city. If my disguise didn't work, I'd have to figure out another way. And somehow, someway, I had to find a horse. I fingered Kate's handgun in my pocket. I would use it if I had to.

The moon hung round and white, and I was both glad and resentful. The bright moon would help once I was in the dark countryside, but right now it shone too brightly.

I stayed in the shadows as much as I could until I reached the sentinels. They stood guard, their bayonets shiny in the moonlight. To my right, the Cooper River gleamed.

Other red-coated soldiers milled about. I stepped among them, hoping to slip unnoticed past the guards. But it was not so easy. "You there!" a guard called to me. "Name and regiment?"

"Butcher Tarleton," I said. "Of the Slaughter Regiment."

As the guard frowned in confusion, I took off running. "Stop him!" the guard screamed.

I veered to the right, the soldiers on my heels. The Cooper River loomed before me, a dark and mysterious abyss.

I took a deep breath and plunged into the water.

CHAPTER 16

REBEL SNAKE

Bullets pinged the surface of the river as I kicked away. None of the soldiers dove in after me. I realized with a smile that the lousy rascals couldn't swim.

I'd never swum so hard and fast in my life. The heavy coat weighed me down. I wriggled free of it and let it float behind me. When I came up for a gulp of air, I looked back.

The soldiers were firing at the bright red coat. I giggled and dove under again, swimming hard against the current.

When I could no longer hear gunshots, I rose to the surface. All was quiet. I was safe for now, but I needed to hurry.

I paddled to the riverbank and paused to catch

my breath. I was drenched, but the summer air was warm. Grinning at my trickery, I made my way along the riverbank.

And then, my smile fell. The handgun had been in my coat pocket. And now it was at the bottom of the river. But I couldn't turn back now. I trudged on, staying clear of the road and the redcoat patrols.

The hot, humid night air of the low country closed around me. Mosquitoes swirled about my face. I walked along the spongy ground, my feet sinking into the marshy soil with each step. At this pace, I'd never find William. I'd be too late to warn him or Marion.

I needed a horse.

I had to come up with a plan. Fast.

Bits of hanging moss clung to my face, and I shivered as I wiped the moss away. *Don't be scared*, I told myself. But I was. The swamps were silent and eerie. Suddenly I longed for the city sounds of Charles Town.

A long strand of moss clung to my leg. I reached down to pull myself free. And then I froze.

It wasn't moss wrapping itself around me. It was a snake.

Golden and brown stripes lined its back. A cottonmouth. Poisonous.

Stay still, I told myself. I'd come across many snakes

on the plantation. I knew that if I stood motionless, the snake would eventually slither away.

I stared down at the cottonmouth, waiting for it to open its jaws and bare its white, cottony mouth.

Then I laughed. This was no cottonmouth. It was a banded water snake. Harmless.

"Hello there," I murmured. "You rebel snake."

As I said the words, an idea sprang to my mind. I laughed again and lowered my arm. As if on command, the snake slithered around my wrist. I grasped its head firmly between my thumb and forefinger, then set off for the road.

Just off to the side of the road, I spotted a live oak with a low-hanging branch. One-armed, I climbed up, careful not to drop the snake, and waited.

I didn't have to wait long. A rumble of hooves soon filled the air, and two red-coated soldiers appeared.

As they passed below me, I shook a branch.

"Whoa!" one soldier said, pulling on his reins to halt the horse. He looked up.

I caught his eye, grinned, and dropped the snake right onto his face.

The soldier screamed and fell from the saddle. Seizing the moment, I swung from the branch, leaped onto the horse, and kicked it into a gallop.

The other soldier gave chase, but I'd gotten a good lead. I led the horse off the road and deep into the trees. Hooves clattered back and forth on the road. The soldier couldn't find me.

I waited, soothing the panting horse. When all was quiet, I nudged the horse through the trees and back onto the road. My heart pounded. If I were caught, I'd not only be a traitor, but also a horse thief.

I'd be hanged for sure.

I journeyed on under the lightening sky. I had to find William, or Marion, before daybreak. If I didn't, I'd certainly be caught.

I rode on. Then I saw a familiar curve in the road. I was near Belle Oak. My plantation. My home.

Spurring the horse to a canter, I turned down the lane.

No grand house stood at the end of the lane. Only a charred pile of bricks. The home I'd grown up in was gone.

"No!" I sobbed quietly into the horse's mane. Tears leaked down my cheeks. Then I sat up, biting my trembling lip.

I was more determined than ever. I must help defeat the British. At any cost.

CHAPTER 17

RETURN HOME

I steered the horse through the familiar paths of the plantation. Despite my determination, my doubts grew. I'd been foolish to think I could find William or Marion. If Tarleton, an experienced soldier, couldn't find them, how could I?

"Stop right there!" a voice called.

Several men stepped in front of me, blocking the path and aiming their guns at me. Militiamen.

I sighed with relief. "I've been looking for you!" I cried. "I've come with a message . . ."

The men didn't lower their guns. "Do tell!" one of them said. Another chuckled.

Fear crawled up my spine. I had heard the chuckle

before. These were certainly the same soldiers who had captured my father. British soldiers. Disguised as Patriot militia.

I whirled the horse about, but more soldiers filled the road behind me. I was trapped.

"Where did you get that horse, young man?" The chuckling soldier was now stern.

I lifted my chin. "I stole it," I said. "And don't you know your manners? You must bow when speaking to a lady."

He frowned. Then his eyes widened. He fell to the ground just as a gunshot rang through the air.

My horse reared in the chaos of gunfire, and I slid to the ground and rolled away quickly into the ditch. When I peered up, I saw dozens of militiamen charging from the trees, firing at the disguised soldiers.

In mere seconds, the outnumbered British threw their weapons to the ground and raised their arms in defeat.

I raised myself to my elbows and saw a pair of boots striding toward me. "Well, well," the man said. "We meet again, Miss Margaret."

I stared up at the face of Francis Marion. His dark eyes twinkled.

Flushed with embarrassment, I sat up and wiped

my dirty face. "I beg pardon, sir," I said, "but will you help me up?"

Marion gave a roaring laugh and pulled me to my feet. "I see you've brought me a horse," he said. "Anything else?"

Quickly, I told him about Tarleton's plans. As I spoke, I scanned the militiamen. No William.

When I finished speaking, Marion nodded. "This information will prove very useful," he said. "We'll be one step ahead of the old Butcher."

"Is there a boy among you named William?" I asked. "He left Charles Town a few days ago to meet up with you."

"William? Yes, a fine boy. Come to our camp."

We marched along marshy paths, the British prisoners in tow, until we reached Marion's camp.

William's jaw gaped when he saw me. I gave him a fierce hug. I told him about Aunt Kate's spying and how I'd outsmarted the British along the Cooper River.

"Belle Oak is gone," I told him, fighting back tears.

William nodded. "I know. Thomas's militia did everything they could, but . . ."

"I don't blame him," I interrupted. "I blame the awful British!"

"Don't worry," William said, trying to calm me.

"The war will be over soon. And then you can rebuild the plantation."

I sank to the ground next to a dwindling campfire. The early morning sun filtered through the cypress leaves. "Did you know about Aunt Kate's spying?" I asked William.

William sat down next to me. "I had my suspicions," he said.

I remembered the day in the cellar, how William had kept eyeing Kate.

Marion came toward us. I noticed he walked with a slight limp. "You've done a fine job, Miss Margaret," he said.

"I'm just the messenger," I said. "I couldn't have done it without Cora and Aunt Kate. They're the real heroes."

"I'm not sure how to repay you," Marion went on.

"My father is a British prisoner," I told him. "Can you help him?"

"Of course," Marion said. "I'll arrange for his release. And if the British don't comply, I'll break him out myself!"

I thanked him.

"Now," Marion continued, "we need to get you to safety. Eliza Lucas Pinckney will take you in. She's staying at her daughter's plantation to wait out the war."

Eliza Lucas, my idol. With a sinking heart, I remembered Kate's whispered words. I realized what she'd meant. She thought she was dying, and she wanted to send me to Eliza Lucas.

"Maggie will love that!" William told Marion.

"No," I said. "I want to go back to Charles Town. To Aunt Kate."

William stared at me, surprised. "But Eliza Lucas is your idol!"

"I want to go to Aunt Kate," I repeated firmly. "She's ill, and I want to be there to care for her." I paused, and then added in a choked voice, "She means so much to me."

"It's a bit risky," Marion said. "But I can arrange transport. From now on, you must promise to be a good Loyalist girl like your aunt."

"I can do that!" I told him with a smile. I knew that even though Kate was a Patriot, she would still try to turn me into a proper lady. And I would just have to put up with it.

Marion ushered me to a small skiff. Two elderly men, dressed as peddlers, would sail me down the river.

I waved goodbye to William and we set off. Exhausted, I lay in the bottom of the boat and drifted to sleep.

I woke to see the spires of St. Michael's Church shining on the horizon. Charles Town, and Cora and Aunt Kate, awaited me. Home. At last I was home.

ABOUT THE AUTHOR

Jessica Gunderson grew up in the small town of Washburn, North Dakota. She has a bachelor's degree from the University of North Dakota and an MFA in Creative Writing from Minnesota State University, Mankato. She has written more than fifty books for young readers. Her book *Ropes of Revolution* won the 2008 Moonbeam Award for best graphic novel. She currently lives in Madison, Wisconsin, with her husband and cat.

MAKING CONNECTIONS

1. What is the theme of this story? What details from the story support the theme?

2. This story is told in the first person point of view. How would it be different if it were told in third person? Why do you think the author chose to tell it in first person?

3. What do you think the main conflict of the story is? Was this conflict resolved?

4. What genre is this novel? What characteristics make it this genre?

5. Choose a character from the story and explain how he or she changes throughout the novel.

6. What happens to Maggie after the war has ended? Write an epilogue that gives insight into Maggie's future.

GLOSSARY

admonished (ad-MON-ishd)—warned or advised someone of his or her faults

allegiance (uh-LEE-junss)—loyal support for someone or something

bayonet (BAY-uh-net)—a long knife that can be fastened to the end of a rifle

dejectedly (di-JEK-tid-lee)—in a sad and depressed manner

delirious (di-LIHR-ee-uhss)—unable to think straight either because of an illness or extreme happiness

dispatching (diss-PACH-ing)—sending something or somebody off

inherit (in-HAIR-it)—to receive money, property, or a title from someone who has died

militia (muh-LISH-uh)—a group of citizens who are trained to fight but who only serve in a time of emergency

nary (NAIR-ee)—not any

nonchalantly (non-shuh-LAHNT-lee)—in a calm and relaxed manner

obligation (ob-luh-GAY-shuhn)—something that is your duty to do

persuade (pur-SWADE)—to succeed in making someone do or believe something by giving the person good reasons

pillagers (PIL-lij-ers)—people who take goods and possessions with ruthless violence

plagued (PLAYGD)—troubled or annoyed

plantation (plan-TAY-shuhn)—a large farm found in warm climates where crops such as coffee, tea, rubber, and cotton are grown

plundering (PLUHN-dur-ing)—stealing things by force

pondering (PON-dur-ing)—thinking about things carefully

raucous (RAW-kuhss)—loud and rowdy

reluctant (ri-LUHK-tuhnt)—showing doubt or unwillingness

replenished (ri-PLEN-ishd)—made full or complete once more

sarcasm (SAR-kaz-uhm)—a remark made usually to hurt someone's feelings or show scorn

sentries (SEN-trees)—people who stand guard and warn others of danger

suitors (SOO-ters)—men who court women or seek to marry them

suspicions (suh-SPISH-uhns)—thoughts, based more on feeling than on fact, that something is wrong or bad

traipsing (TRAYP-sing)—walking or traveling about without a plan or purpose

STRAIGHT FROM HISTORY

American General Benjamin Lincoln
(1733–1810)

At the start of the war, Benjamin Lincoln oversaw the military organization and supplies for the colonies. Eventually, Lincoln came to command troops under George Washington and took part in several important surrenders. In 1780, while in Charleston, South Carolina, Lincoln was forced to surrender to the British in what would be the largest American surrender in the war. But just a year later, Lincoln accepted the British force's surrender at Yorktown, ending the war. After the war, Lincoln continued to play an active role in early American politics.

American Colonel Francis Marion
(1732–1795)

Francis Marion was an officer in the American army. After the Americans forces in South Carolina surrendered, Marion took a group of twenty to seventy men to fight the British forces occupying the state. Because their forces were small, they attacked using ambushes and hit-and-run tactics. This style of fighting, called guerilla warfare, worked well for the Americans. Marion came to be known by the British as the dreaded "swamp fox." After the war, Marion served in South Carolina's state senate.

British Lieutenant Colonel Banastre "The Butcher" Tarleton
(1754–1833)

Although only in his twenties, Banastre Tarleton proved himself to be a dangerous threat to the American troops. The British officer led a powerful cavalry, but he was best known for his brutality. Americans began referring to Tarleton as "The Butcher" after the Battle of Waxhaws, when he ordered his men to shoot American troops after they had surrendered. His actions made Americans rally together to fight such cruelties. Tarleton returned to Britain after the war where he served in Parliament.

Eliza Lucas Pinckney
(1722–1793)

At a young age, Eliza Lucas Pinckney moved with her family from Antigua to Charleston, South Carolina where the family owned a plantation. During her schooling, which took place in England, Pinckney became interested in the study of plants. On the plantation, Pinckney began experimenting with growing indigo, a plant originally from the West Indies from which the precious indigo dye was made. Eventually, Pinckney developed a strand of indigo that could grow in the South Carolina climate, and it became one of the most important pre-Revolution exports. Pinckney continued to experiment with other ventures, including raising silkworms to produce silk.

Read more about the people and events of the Revolutionary War with

CONNECT

Or discover great websites and books like this one at **www.facthound.com.** Just type in the book **ID: 9781434297013** and you're ready to go.